W9-BJU-969

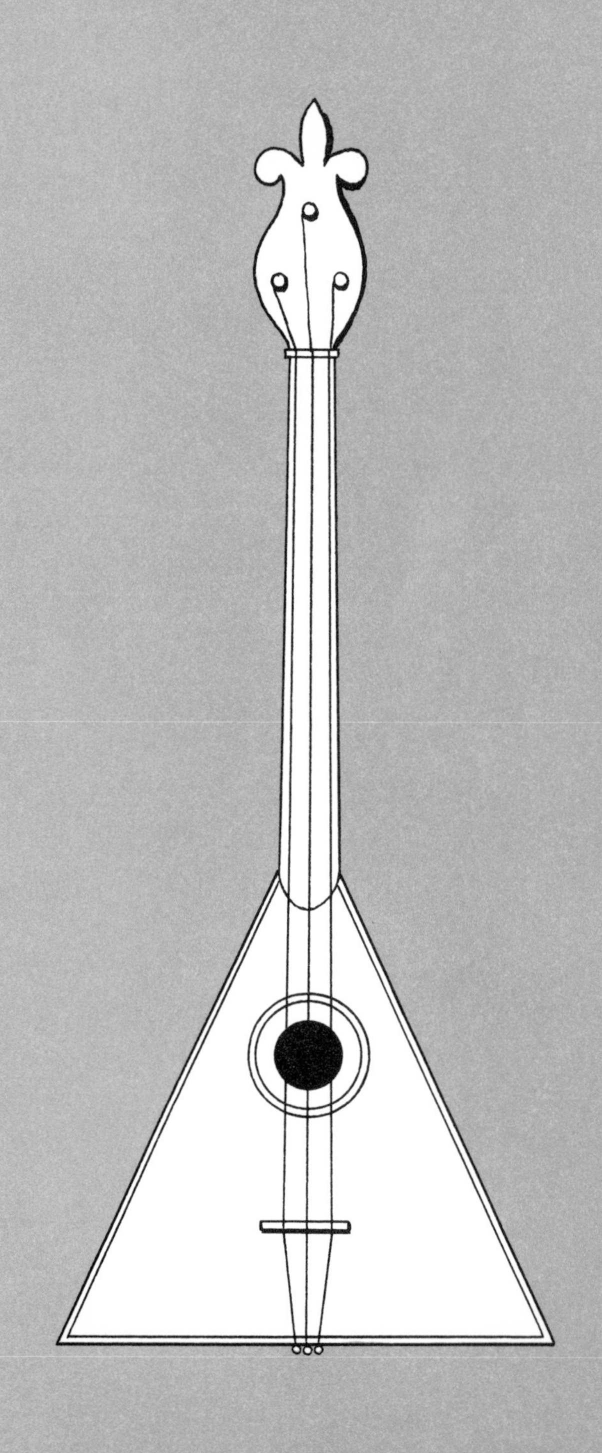

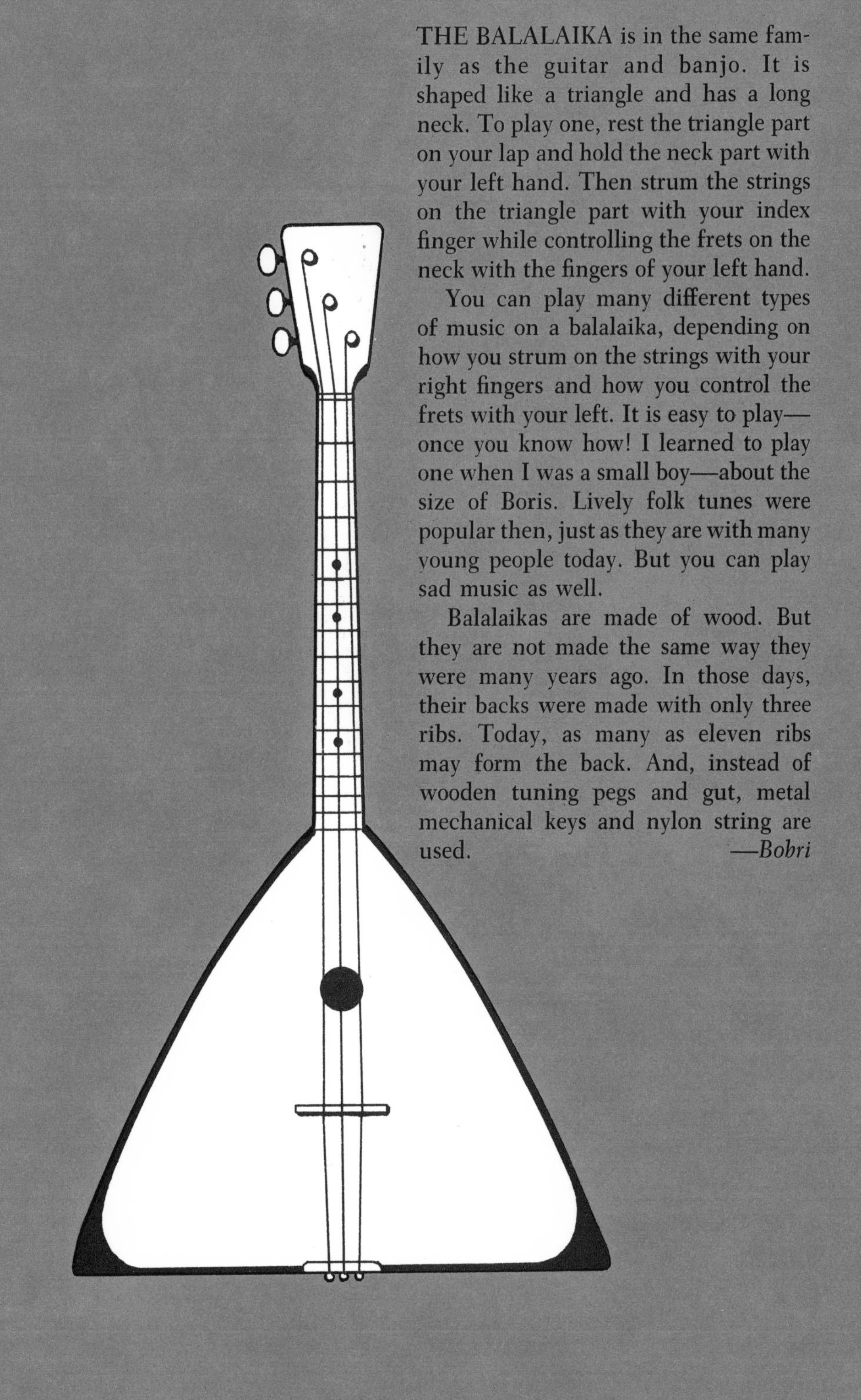

THE BALALAIKA is in the same family as the guitar and banjo. It is shaped like a triangle and has a long neck. To play one, rest the triangle part on your lap and hold the neck part with your left hand. Then strum the strings on the triangle part with your index finger while controlling the frets on the neck with the fingers of your left hand.

You can play many different types of music on a balalaika, depending on how you strum on the strings with your right fingers and how you control the frets with your left. It is easy to play—once you know how! I learned to play one when I was a small boy—about the size of Boris. Lively folk tunes were popular then, just as they are with many young people today. But you can play sad music as well.

Balalaikas are made of wood. But they are not made the same way they were many years ago. In those days, their backs were made with only three ribs. Today, as many as eleven ribs may form the back. And, instead of wooden tuning pegs and gut, metal mechanical keys and nylon string are used. —*Bobri*

Library of Congress Catalogue Card Number: 64-12745

Printed in the United States of America

# HIS BALALAIKA

BY ESPHYR SLOBODKINA

PICTURES BY BOBRI

ABELARD-SCHUMAN
LONDON NEW YORK TORONTO

In a little Russian village of Babayevo, near the City of Ivanovo, lived young Widow Baranova with her small son, Boris. They lived in an old wooden hut, close to the very edge of the village.

It was a poor little hut, dingy from the outside, and almost empty inside: two benches, a table, and a few clay dishes were all that Widow Baranova had. But on the rough wall, just above one of the benches, hung a very fine balalaika. Its smooth, polished wood, its gay silken bow, and, most of all, its slim, delicate shape looked very odd indeed in these poor surroundings. Widow Baranova knew it, and many was the time when she thought of selling the balalaika to buy bread for her little son. But she never could bring herself to part with it—it had belonged to her Husband and, except for her little Boris, it was her only treasure.

When Boris was still very small,
his Mother noticed that he liked to play
with his Father's balalaika.
He would climb upon the bench and reach
for the magic object hanging on the wall.
As he plucked the strings one by one,
Boris would laugh happily
at the pretty sounds they made.
Widow Baranova was afraid
that the boy might break the balalaika,
and yet she could not forbid him to touch it.
So, instead, she taught Boris to treat
it with the greatest of care.

Widow Baranova worked very hard to earn a living for her little son and for herself. In the early autumn she helped the peasants to harvest wheat and hay. In the winter she embroidered linen and made lace for the towels of rich men's daughters.

And all spring and summer long she gathered flowers, berries, and mushrooms, put them into little birch-bark baskets, and sold them on Market Days in the City of Ivanovo.

As the years went by, Boris grew to be a fine, strong boy. He was a good, dutiful son to his Mother, and never refused to do anything she asked him to do. But Boris loved his balalaika, and

spent hours playing and singing all the songs he could learn. Widow Baranova was very proud of her son's gift, so she often let him play and sing instead of asking him to fetch some water from the well or to chop some wood for the stove.

The villagers watched the mother and son, shook their heads, and said that nothing good could come of it. At last, Widow Baranova's friends went to her, and said: "Boris is a big, strong fellow now. Why don't you send him out to work so that he can help you to earn your living?"

So, Boris went out to look for work.
Before long he found a Rich
Peasant who was willing to hire him.
But, no matter how hard Boris
tried, everything went wrong:
When he tried to help with ploughing,
he made crooked furrows.
When he tried to help with sowing,
the wind scattered all the grain
in the opposite direction.
And when he tried to milk a cow,
she wouldn't stand still for him.
She just kicked the milk
pail over, and walked away.
The Rich Peasant
became furious.
He scolded Boris for
being a lazy
good-for-nothing,
and chased him away
waving a big stick
at him.

Boris was very upset. He did not know what to do. So he did what he always did whenever he was sad: he went home, took down his Father's balalaika and played a plaintive tune.

"Never mind, my Little Pigeon," said his Mother. "Tomorrow we shall go to gather mushrooms, flowers and berries. The two of us will gather twice as much, and together we will bring twice as much money from the Market."

Early next morning Boris and his Mother went into the woods. "You go this way, and I'll go that way," said Widow Baranova, "and in the evening we will meet at this very spot by the old tree stump."
"Mind you, fill your baskets to the brim!" she added.
Boris and his Mother went their separate ways.
All day long they worked very hard filling their little baskets with flowers, mushrooms and berries.
But in the evening when they met again, Widow Baranova took one look at her son's baskets, and began to cry. The baskets were full enough, to be sure. But the berries were too ripe to sell, the flowers were common weeds, and the mushrooms were poisonous toadstools!
"What am I, a poor widow, to do with a useless son like that?" she said time and time again through her tears.

Boris was miserable.
What his Mother said was true—he was useless.
So, when he came home, once again he took
down the balalaika, and played the most plaintive
tune he knew.

That night Boris could not sleep at all.
He kept thinking of his Mother and of how he could help her. But every time he thought of a job he might try to get, he remembered the Rich Peasant and his words: "good-for-nothing." The longer he thought about it, the more dejected he felt.
"Well," he said to himself, "if I cannot help, at least I can stop being a burden to her.
I know what I'll do—
I'll run away, and become a soldier."

His mind made up, Boris packed a little bundle, kissed his sleeping Mother good-bye, and before the sun was up, began to walk toward the City of Ivanovo.

In the City of Ivanovo
Boris tried to become
a soldier, but:
"You are too young!"
said the Sergeant of the Army.
"You are too weak!"
said the Captain of the Navy.
"You couldn't even fit on a
horse!" said the Cossacks,
and they laughed long and
loudly at their own joke.

Feeling more useless than ever, Boris trudged
on his way home. When he came back,
his Mother did not ask him any questions.
She just put a bowl of cabbage soup and
a thick slice of rye bread on the table
for his supper, and went to bed.
But Boris did not feel very hungry.
Late into the night he sat
on the steps of his hut
playing one plaintive
tune after another
on his Father's
balalaika, until
he was so tired he fell asleep right there,
leaning against the doorpost.

Boris was still asleep when he felt his Mother shake him, and heard her say: "Wake up, wake up, Boris! I think I have good news for you! I hear Ivan, the old Cowherd, needs a helper. If you hurry up and get there first, maybe they will hire you!"
Boris did not waste any time. He ran all the way to the Village Green. Seeing that he wanted the job so badly, and because he was Widow Baranova's son, the Village Elders agreed to make Boris the Cowherd's helper.

At last Boris had work which was just right for him.
He made a fine helper for old Ivan:
He had a sharp eye to see a cow, no matter where she strayed.
And he had a sharp ear to hear the cry of a young calf from no matter where he was lost.
But, best of all, he had a sweet voice and swift fingers to sing songs and to play his balalaika. It made long hours seem short, and hard work seem easy.

Everybody agreed that Boris was a very good cowherd.
But everybody still looked down their noses at
young Boris, for being a cowherd was about as low
a job as one could have in a Russian village.
But Boris did not care. It is true that his Mother
often sighed about their poverty, but she did not
really mind it because Boris seemed to be so happy.
And he was. Nobody could now say that he was lazy,
and best of all, he had all the time he wanted
to play his balalaika!

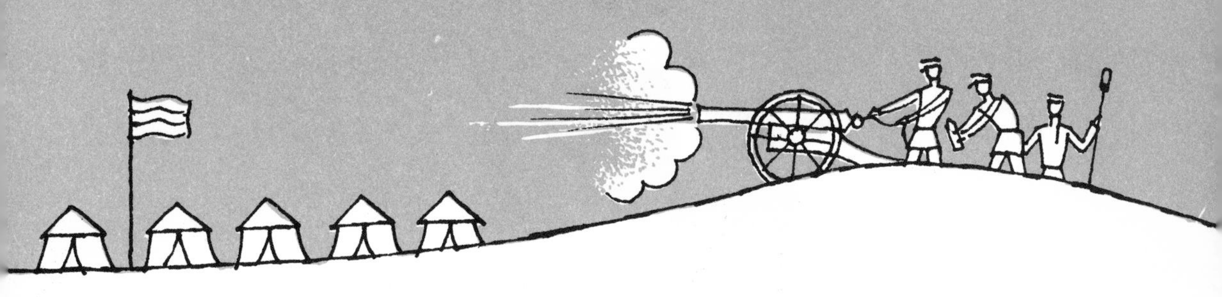

Just about this time, The Commander-in-Chief of all Russian Armies decided that it was time for his soldiers, for his officers, and for his generals to have some war exercises. So, off went the generals in different directions. The officers rushed hither and thither on their magnificent chargers. And the soldiers marched over the hills and down the dales in long, orderly columns.
They pitched tents, and they broke camp.
They shot from cannons, and they did some target shooting with their rifles.
They attacked shouting "Ho-o-rr-a-y!!!"
and they retreated in perfect order.
Altogether they were very fine war exercises,
and just what the Commander-in-Chief had ordered.

One day, it happened that a Very Important General
made his camp near the village of Babayevo.
No sooner were the tents up than the General sent
several young officers to tell the villagers to
bring provisions for him and his soldiers.
The officers galloped off, and told the Village
Elders that their General would stand for no
nonsense: everybody had to give something to
their Country, their Soldiers, and their General.
The villagers knew that when a general said
"no nonsense," he meant "no nonsense."
But when an Important General like that
said "no nonsense," he really meant:
"NO NONSENSE!!!"
So, without any fuss, all of the villagers
brought in something:
Some brought a sack of flour;
some brought a sack of potatoes.
Some brought a suckling pig;
and some brought a little lamb.
Everybody gave something to their Country, their
Soldiers, and to their General. That is, everybody
except Widow Baranova and her son, Boris. "I am
only a poor cowherd, and I have nothing to give,"
said Boris.

The officers rattled their sabres and stamped their boots, they were so angry. Then they bound Boris hand and foot, and brought him in front of the Very Important General.

"Your Excellency," said the eldest of the young officers, clicking his heels and saluting the General, "this miserable creature claims he has nothing to give."

"Eh?" said the General, his fearsome whiskers bristling up almost to his eyebrows.

"What sort of a person is he if he has nothing to give to his Country, his Soldiers, and especially to his General?" "You are not a beggar, are you?"

"No, Sir," replied Boris, "but I am only the village cowherd, and as everybody knows, my poor widowed mother and I must live on what others see fit to give us."

"Oh?" said the General. This time it was his eyebrows that went up. "You must be very unhappy being so poor."

"No, Sir," answered Boris. "Not at all. I have my work, and I have my fun. I mind the cows, and the cows don't mind if I play my balalaika. . . .

Matter of fact, if Your Excellency would permit me to say so, I think they like it, for they never stray far away from me."
"Ah-ha!" roared His Excellency, the General. "So, you think you can play the balalaika? Silence! Never mind the answer! We will soon find out. Sergeant! Bring the boy's balalaika, and be quick about it!"

The Sergeant galloped off to Widow Baranova's
poor little hut. He paid no attention to her tears
and to her pleading questions about her young son.
He simply took the balalaika off the wall,
put it across his saddle, and galloped
away back to the camp.

"Untie him!" shouted the General. "And now, let the little whippersnapper show me what he can do!" he growled, staring fiercely at Boris.

Boris began to play. First he played some plaintive tunes, but noticed that the General grew very sad. So, he tried to cheer him up,

and played some gay tunes. The General began to smile. And when Boris started playing some dance tunes, the General began to clap his hands and to stamp his foot to mark the time.

He grew so gay, he ordered his soldiers and the villagers who gathered about to make a circle so that some young men and girls could dance for him. The General was in such a happy mood, he ordered a big feast and invited everybody to stay and celebrate with him.

Altogether, it turned out to be a wonderful day, and everybody who knew the General said that they never saw him in such fine spirits.

Later in the evening, when all the villagers had
gone home, and the camp fires were burning low,
Boris played some marching songs.
All the soldiers, all the officers, and even
the General himself
joined in the singing.
They made a wonderful chorus.
"Ah, Boris, my boy! You have talent!
Real talent!" sighed the General.
He was silent for a while. "Ah-ha!" he roared
suddenly, slapping himself on the forehead.
"I have it! You must stay with us so that you
can play for us always!"
"B-but," stammered Boris,
"I was told I'm too young to join the Army."
"N O N S E N S E ! ! !"
roared the General still louder,
"I O R D E R you to join the Army!"

And that is how it happened that young Boris
and his balalaika joined the Army.
Forever after, they rode on a beautiful black horse,
all decked out with bright ribbons,
and whenever the going got too tough,
or the men became dispirited, or
the General felt sad, Boris would strike up a song.
In no time at all everybody would join in a happy
chorus, and feel better again.
Widow Baranova stayed on in the village of
Babayevo, but she was never poor again for Boris
never forgot to send most of his pay to his Mother.
She could buy anything she needed, and so she did.
But her greatest treasure was something
which no money could buy.
It was a picture of her young son, Boris,
sitting on a beautiful black horse,
playing his famous balalaika.

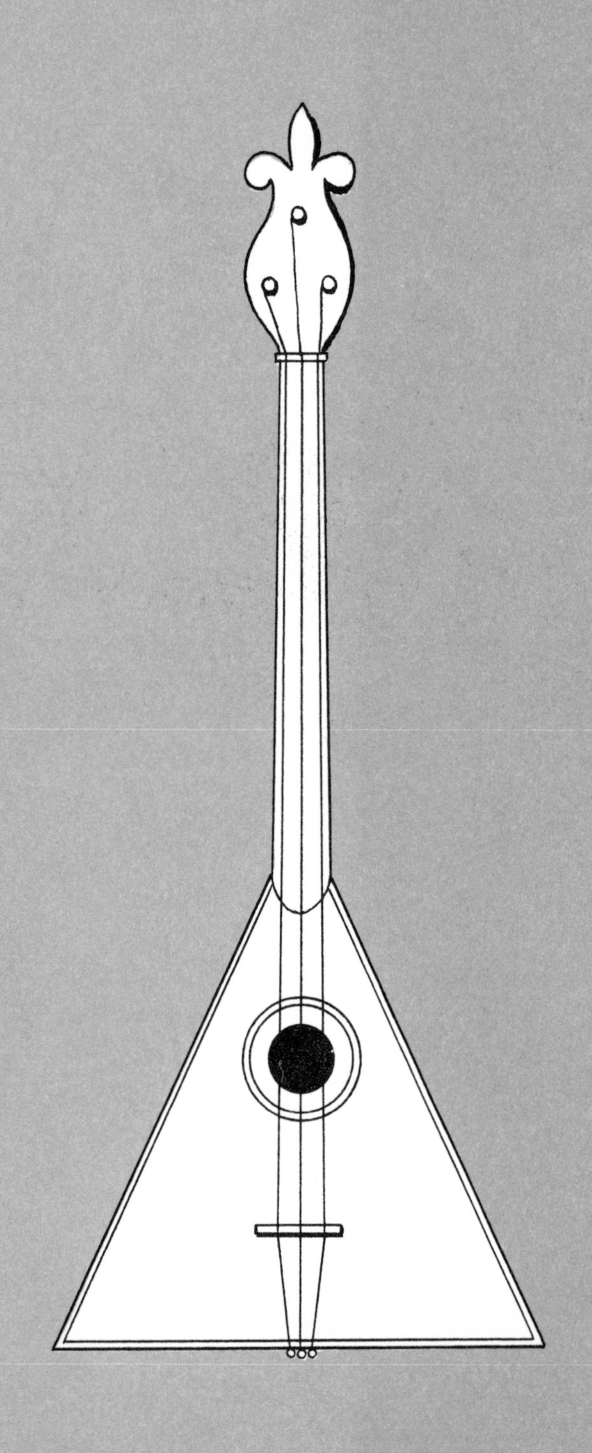

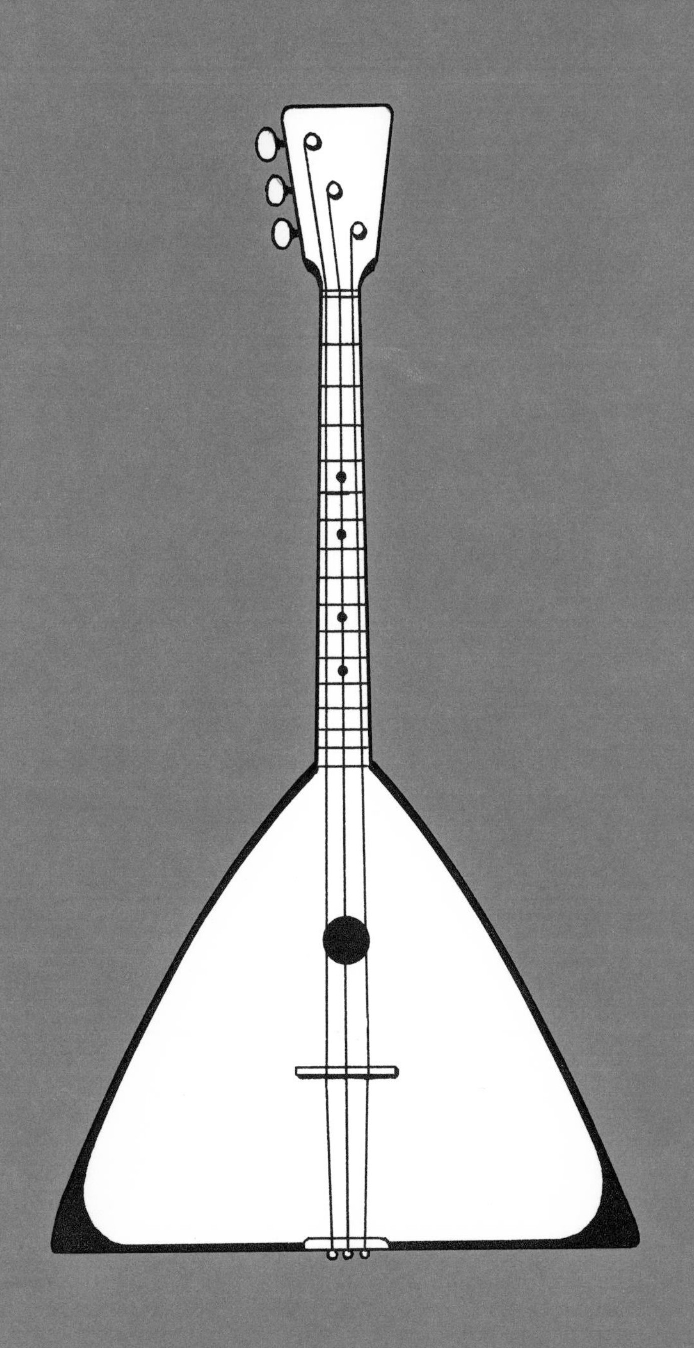